In loving memory of my father, HARRY MINSKY, who created the character of Ruffy Butchbang and told stories about Ruffy to all the children in the neighborhood. His specialty was adding special sound effects that the children loved to hear. And in loving memory of my brother, SAM MINSKY, who was a wonderful artist and who wanted to be a cartoonist and illustrator but never had the opportunity to follow his dream.

www.mascotbooks.com

COOL KIDS

For more information, please contact:

Mascot Books

620 Herndon Parkway, Suite 320

Herndon, VA 20170

info@mascotbooks.com

Library of Congress Control Number: 2021906151

CPSIA Code: PRT0221A

ISBN-13: 978-1-64543-697-3

Printed in the United States

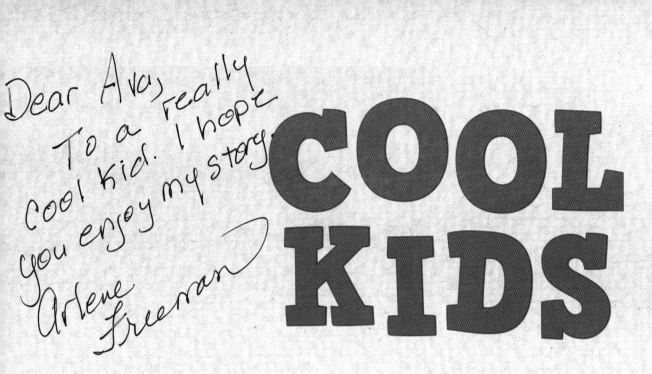

Dear Ava,
To a really
cool kid. I hope
you enjoy my story.
Arlene Freeman

COOL KIDS

Written by
Arlene Freeman

Illustrated by Amelina Jones

This is Michael Goodly, and he lives with his mom, dad, sister Vera, and his dog Cooper in a house in New Jersey. His house has a big backyard where he likes to play football with his friends and Cooper.

One day, as he relaxed in bed with Cooper, Michael thought about the big change that would be happening the next day:

Tomorrow, I will be going to a new school!

My old school only went up to the third grade.
I am going into the fourth grade and my friends are coming too.
I'm ready for the big day!

The next day, Michael's mom greeted him with his favorite breakfast in the kitchen, saying, "Good morning, Michael. Today's the big day, your first day at a new school!"

"I'm ready!" said Michael.

"Hurry, Michael. You don't want to be late! Ted, Eric, and Todd are here," his mom announced after he licked his plate clean. "Bye, mom!" replied Michael. He patted Cooper on his head one last time, and then waved goodbye.

When they arrived at school, Michael and his friends began to talk about the coming year. "Do you think we'll be able to make the football team? Last year, we were the big guys and now we might be the little guys," said Eric, as he tossed a football.

"Don't worry. Things will be great because we are in the same class," said Ted.

Two weeks in school had passed, and Michael's mom wanted to check in. "How are you liking your new school, Michael?" Michael replied, "I like my classes. We have fun painting, singing, and learning new things every day. I have two new friends named Axi and Nicole. I am always there to help them when they have trouble, but I just wish I was playing football like I did at my old school."

"Don't worry, things will work out,"

said his mom.

The next day at school, Michael saw a group of boys playing football and wanted to join them. "Hi guys," said Michael.

"Go away, kid! We don't want any wimpy kids here!" yelled one of the boys in the group.

"I'm not a wimpy kid!" yelled Michael.

"Come on, Ruffy. Let's play ball!" exclaimed another boy, ignoring Michael.

I know that name. It is a funny name—Ruffy Butchbang. He's the one who is always so loud in class and acts like a tough guy. He has lots of friends who follow him around. Maybe if I follow them around, they will notice me and let me play ball with them, thought Michael.

Not long after that, Michael saw Ruffy and his gang pushing other kids out of the way in order to get to the front of the lunch line.

"Hey! I was here first!" yelped the kid at the front of the line.

"NOT ANYMORE!"

yelled Ruffy.

Michael saw Ted coming toward him eating some candy. Before Michael could call out to him, Ruffy ran up and pulled the candy right out of Ted's hand. "Look, guys! Want some candy?" Ruffy yelled mockingly.

Maybe I should start doing stuff like that in order to impress Ruffy, thought Michael.

Oh, here comes Todd, Michael thought, right before deciding to put his foot out and trip his friend.

"Why did you do that?" yelled Todd.

"Because I wanted to!" Michael shouted, just loud enough for Ruffy to notice. Todd got up and ran away, hurt by Michael's decision to trip him. Inside, Michael thought, *I hope Todd is okay.*

Every day, Michael saw Ruffy and his gang playing football. Wanting to play with them, Michael acted like a tough guy in order to get Ruffy to notice him. Eventually, Ruffy did.

"Wanna play ball, kid?" called Ruffy.

"Sure!" yelled Michael, and off he went to join his new friends.

One weekend, Michael was on his way to his room and passed by a mirror in the hallway, stopping short when he noticed something in his reflection.

WHAT! WHO IS THAT? wondered Michael. He looked again, touching his face. *Is this me?* he thought. *What is happening to me?* His face was wrinkled, he had black eyes, and he was completely covered in blue dots. Cooper growled at him and hid under the bed.

> *Why is this happening to me?*
> *Does everyone see me like this?*
> Michael panicked.

The next day at school, no one seemed to notice the change, which relieved Michael.

Oh, there's Axi, thought Michael. Michael greeted his friend by saying, "Hi, stupid!" Axi ran away crying, which made Ruffy laugh. Michael then saw Nicole and said, "Hi, dumbbell!" Ruffy heard it all.

"You're a cool kid. Want to play football with us after school?" Ruffy asked.

"Sure!" said Michael, excitedly.

That afternoon, when Michael came home from school and looked in the mirror, his appearance had gotten worse. His teeth had turned black, which really frightened him. Cooper growled at him and ran away.

He looked meaner than he ever had before.

Michael sat on his bed and cried. *What have I done to make me look like this?* thought Michael. *Cooper won't come near me. Eric, Todd, Teddy, and even Axi and Nicole won't talk to me anymore. Did I scare them away?*

Michael thought about it for a minute and then realized it was because of how he had been treating them. He was becoming a bully just like Ruffy Butchbang and his friends. Michael was so sad. He missed all of his friends. Ruffy and his gang weren't his real friends—they were just bullies who hurt people. They thought they were tough and tried to scare people that they thought were weak. Inside, they were really the weak ones.

W hen Michael saw Todd at school
the next day, he apologized to him.

"I am so sorry that I tripped you. It was mean.
Can we be friends again?" asked Michael.

"Sure," agreed Todd.

Later, Michael saw Axi and Nicole in class.

"I'm so sorry that I said those mean things to you both. I know you are smart, Axi, and you are fun to be around, Nicole. I was trying to be cool by calling you names, but I was just being mean. Will you be my friends again?" asked Michael.

"Sure, Michael! We are so happy! We missed you so much," they responded.

Michael also patched things up with Eric and Ted.

"You are my friends, which means that we should help each other and always be nice," said Michael. Eric and Ted agreed, shaking Michael's hand.

When Michael passed by the mirror that night,

he noticed a change.

He had turned back into the old Michael!
The dots were gone, his teeth white again,
and his wrinkles had disappeared.

Cooper jumped up and started licking him, which made Michael smile. Michael finally felt good about himself. He knew that he was a good kid and did not have to prove himself to anyone, especially to a bully like Ruffy Butchbang. Michael was already cool because he was a nice kid and a good friend. Hopefully someday, Ruffy Butchbang would become just as cool as Michael.

The next day, Michael asked Ted, Eric, and Todd to play football, but they needed more players. Before long, Max and Quinn came along to ask if they could join. "Come on!" yelled Michael gladly.

Then, the strangest thing happened! Out of the corner of his eye, Michael saw Ruffy and his gang watching them play football. Ruffy then started coming toward Michael.

"We're going to play too," said Ruffy.

"NO, YOU ARE NOT!" yelled Michael, standing up to him. "You have bullied all of my friends and they don't want to play with you."

Ruffy went back to his gang and seemed to be discussing something with them. He then turned around and started coming back toward Michael.

"We are sorry for being so mean. Is there any way that we can all be friends?" asked Ruffy. Michael went back to his friends and they agreed: "Let's all be friends!" they yelled happily.

Michael took Ruffy aside and said, "You know, Ruffy, being a tough guy doesn't always make you feel good inside. Trust me, it doesn't make you cool, either. You can be cool and have lots of friends by just being nice and helping others. Your friends will really like you better that way," said Michael.

"I think that's exactly what I will do!" exclaimed Ruffy.

"What is your real name, Ruffy?" asked Michael.

"It's Gerald," replied Ruffy hesitantly.

"Well, come on, Jerry! Let's play ball!" yelled Michael.

THE
END

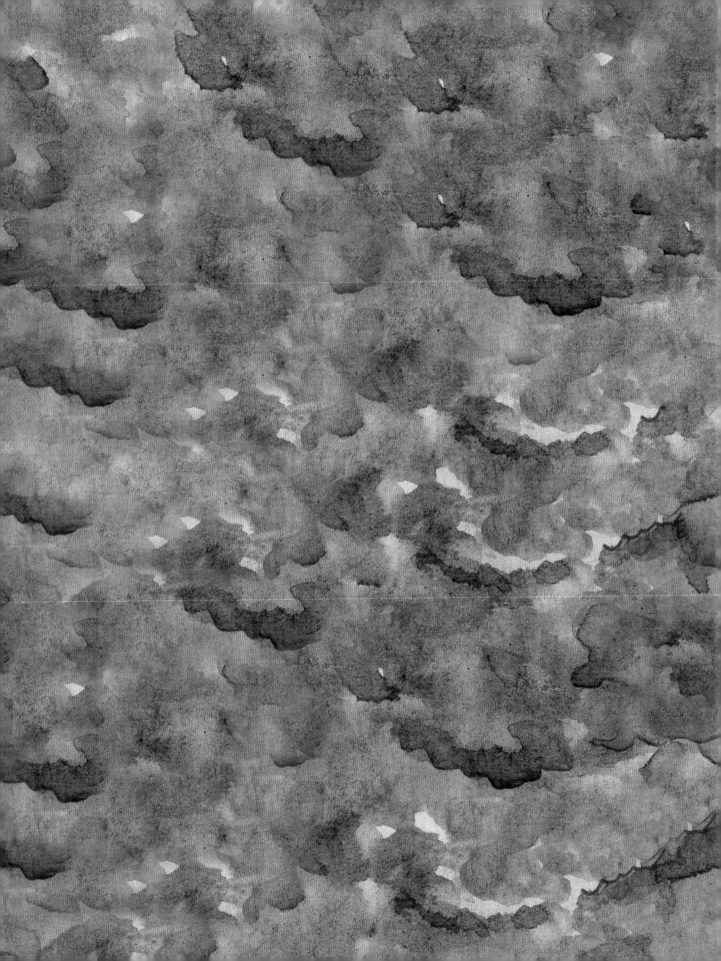

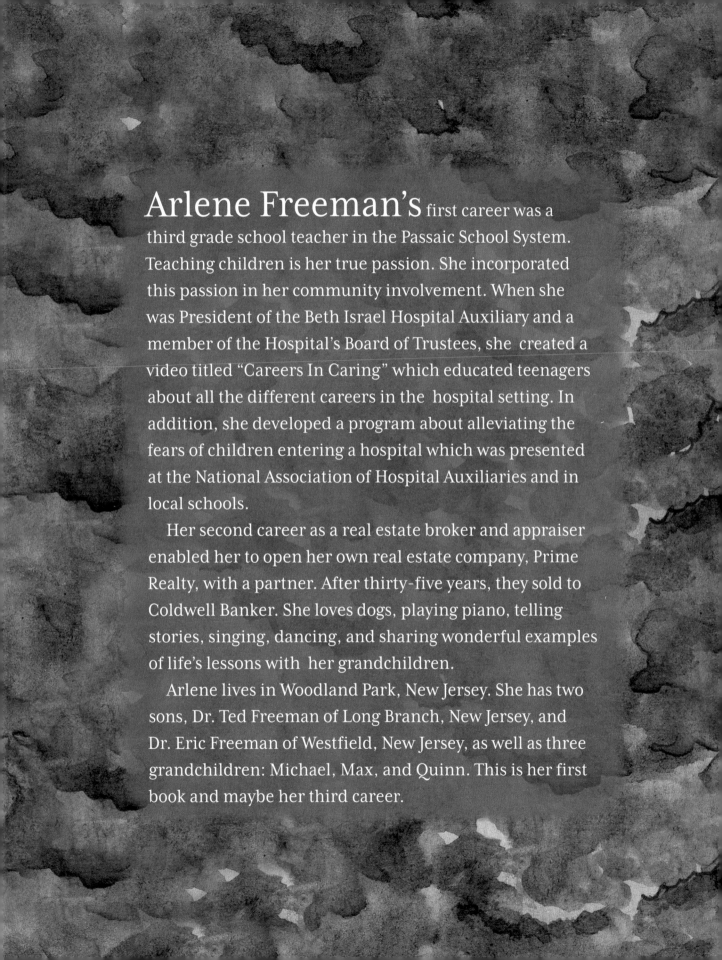

Arlene Freeman's first career was a third grade school teacher in the Passaic School System. Teaching children is her true passion. She incorporated this passion in her community involvement. When she was President of the Beth Israel Hospital Auxiliary and a member of the Hospital's Board of Trustees, she created a video titled "Careers In Caring" which educated teenagers about all the different careers in the hospital setting. In addition, she developed a program about alleviating the fears of children entering a hospital which was presented at the National Association of Hospital Auxiliaries and in local schools.

Her second career as a real estate broker and appraiser enabled her to open her own real estate company, Prime Realty, with a partner. After thirty-five years, they sold to Coldwell Banker. She loves dogs, playing piano, telling stories, singing, dancing, and sharing wonderful examples of life's lessons with her grandchildren.

Arlene lives in Woodland Park, New Jersey. She has two sons, Dr. Ted Freeman of Long Branch, New Jersey, and Dr. Eric Freeman of Westfield, New Jersey, as well as three grandchildren: Michael, Max, and Quinn. This is her first book and maybe her third career.